# Max and Zoe

## The Very Best Art Project

by Shelley Swanson Sateren

illustrated by Mary Sullivan

PICTURE WINDOW BOOKS
a capstone imprint

Max and Zoe is published by Picture Window Books,
A Capstone Imprint
1710 Roe Crest Drive
North Mankato, Minnesota 56003
www.capstonepub.com

Copyright © 2014 Picture Window Books

Library of Congress Cataloging-in-Publication Data
Sateren, Shelley Swanson.
 Max and Zoe : the very best art project / by Shelley Swanson
Sateren; illustrated by Mary Sullivan.
     p. cm. -- (Max and Zoe)
 Summary: When Zoe has trouble drawing a self-portrait for the
second grade art project, she turns to Max for help.
 ISBN 978-1-4048-7201-1 (library binding)
 ISBN 978-1-4795-2329-0 (paperback)
 1.  Self-portraits--Juvenile fiction. 2.  Drawing--Juvenile fiction.
3.  Helping behavior--Juvenile fiction. 4.  Best friends--Juvenile fiction.
5.  Elementary schools--Juvenile fiction. [1. Self-portraits--Fiction.
2. Drawing--Fiction. 3. Helpfulness--Fiction. 4. Best friends--Fiction.
5. Friendship--Fiction. 6. Elementary schools--Fiction. 7. Schools--
Fiction.] I. Sullivan, Mary, 1958- ill. II. Title. III. Title: Very best art
project. IV. Series: Sateren, Shelley Swanson. Max and Zoe.

 PZ7.S249155Mdv 2013
 813.54--dc23

                                        2012047381

Designer: Kristi Carlson

Printed in the United States      4634

# Table of Contents

It was time for art, which was Zoe's favorite class. Today Zoe saw a giant canvas hanging in the front of the art room.

"What is that thing?" Max asked.

"It is the giant canvas for our self-portrait project! We are finally doing it!" cried Zoe.

"You've been waiting all year for this project," said Max.

Every year, the second grade class painted a giant canvas. It hung in the library.

"For the next two weeks, you'll practice on paper. Then you'll paint your portrait on the canvas," said Mr. Baker, their art teacher.

Mr. Baker drew an oval on the board. With two lines, he divided it into four equal parts.

"Okay," he said. "Let's get our proportions right. Eyes go on this line. The nose goes here."

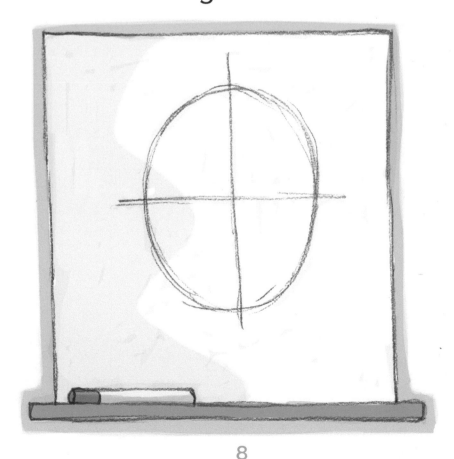

Max listened and watched. Zoe didn't listen or watch. She quickly drew her self-portrait.

"It's not a race, Zoe," whispered Max.

"Mr. Baker always shows my art as the best example," she said. "So I have to get done first."

Mr. Baker finished talking. Zoe bolted over and showed him her drawing.

"I'm done. You can show it to everyone," she said.

"Hmm," he said. "Where should the eyes be?"

Zoe frowned.

"I think you need to start over, Zoe," Mr. Baker said.

Then Mr. Baker held up Max's drawing.

"Look, everyone," he said. "This is a great example of proportion. Good work, Max!"

Zoe threw her drawing in the trash.

The next week, Zoe studied

Mr. Baker's portrait examples.

She studied her face in a mirror,

too. Then she began to draw.

"This looks dumb," she said.

"No it doesn't! Keep going,"
said Max.

Zoe tried her best, but it was
hard. She tried drawing her eyes.

"These don't look right,"
she said.

Max tried to block the trash can.

But Zoe tossed her drawing anyway.

Max said, "You'll get it, Zoe."

So she tried again.

"My ears don't belong there,"

she groaned.

Zoe tore the paper into pieces

and threw them on the table.

"I don't like art anymore,"

she said.

"Don't say that," said Max.

"Keep trying."

"I'm all tried out," said Zoe.

The bell rang and art class was over. Max could draw a perfect self-portrait. Zoe couldn't even draw a nose!

Zoe plopped her head down on her desk and sighed.

## Chapter 3
### The Perfect Portrait

That night, Zoe felt better. She called Max.

"Please come over," she said.
"I need your help."

"I'm on my way," Max said.

Zoe and Max spent every night that week drawing.

Max drew Zoe. Zoe drew Max. Then they worked on drawing their own faces.

Every night, Zoe got better.

Max was a good teacher.

"I think I like art again," Zoe said.

"What a relief!" said Max.

The next day, Mr. Baker said
they would go in alphabetical
order to paint. That meant Zoe
was last.

When Mr. Baker finally called
out Zoe's name, she was ready.

Zoe hurried to the canvas and studied her square. Then she grabbed a brush and painted her self-portrait.

She took her time and did her best.

"Done," she said and grinned. "That's me, all right!"

"It sure is," said Mr. Baker.

"And it's a perfect portrait," said Max.

"I agree," said Zoe.

## About the Author

Shelley Swanson Sateren is the award-winning author of many children's books. She has worked as a children's book editor and in a children's bookstore. Today, besides writing, Shelley works with elementary-school-aged children in various settings. She lives in St. Paul, Minnesota, with her husband and two sons.

## About the Illustrator

Mary Sullivan has been drawing and writing her whole life, which has mostly been spent in Texas. She earned her BFA from the University of Texas in Studio Art, but she considers herself a self-trained illustrator. Mary lives in Cedar Park, a suburb of Austin, Texas.

# Glossary

**canvas (KAN-vuhss)** — thick, strong cloth used to paint on

**divide (duh-VIDE)** — to separate into parts

**feature (FEE-chur)** — any of the different parts of the face

**portrait (POR-trit)** — a picture of a person

**proportion (pruh-POR-shuhn)** — correct size or place of something as it compares to other things

**self-portrait (self-POR-trit)** — a picture of yourself made by yourself

# Discussion Questions

1. Zoe was excited about her art project. Talk about something that you are excited about in your favorite class.

2. Why is it important to watch and listen to your teacher?

3. At the end of the story, Zoe is proud of herself. Talk about a time when you felt proud of yourself.

# Writing Prompts

1. Look in a mirror and study your face's features. List three shapes that you see.

2. What is a skill that you worked hard to learn? Write a few sentences about that skill.

3. What is the best project you ever did in art class? Write down your answer and your reason.

# Make Your Own Portrait

The hardest part of drawing portraits is getting proportion right. You can practice with these fun steps.

**What you need:**

• 1 unlined, 8 x 11-inch sheet of paper

• pencil with eraser

• 1 bowl, about 6 inches wide

• ruler

• crayons, markers, or colored pencils

## What you do:

1. Lay the bowl upside-down in the middle of the paper. Draw around it to make a circle.

2. Using the ruler's edge, draw two crossing lines that divide the circle into four equal parts (see page 8). Draw a small dot where the lines meet.

3. Draw the eyes on the center line. The inside of each eye should be about 1 inch from the center dot.

4. Draw the top of the nose at the center dot. The bottom of the nose should be halfway to the chin. Make the bottom of the nose as wide as the inside of the eyes.

5. Draw the mouth halfway between the chin and the bottom of the nose. Make the mouth as wide as the center of the eyes.

6. Draw the top of the ears at the center line. The bottom of the ears should line up with the bottom of the nose.

7. Erase the lines. Add hair, then color your portrait.